Dedication

This book is lovingly dedicated to
my grandson, Andrew~
who has always been and continues to be a delight
to our family!

Parkway Garden had a big old bird.
BIRD? Well, yes, if bird's the word.

THE BIG OLD TURKEY

By

Terry Phillips Griffin

Illustrated by
Deri Joeliandri

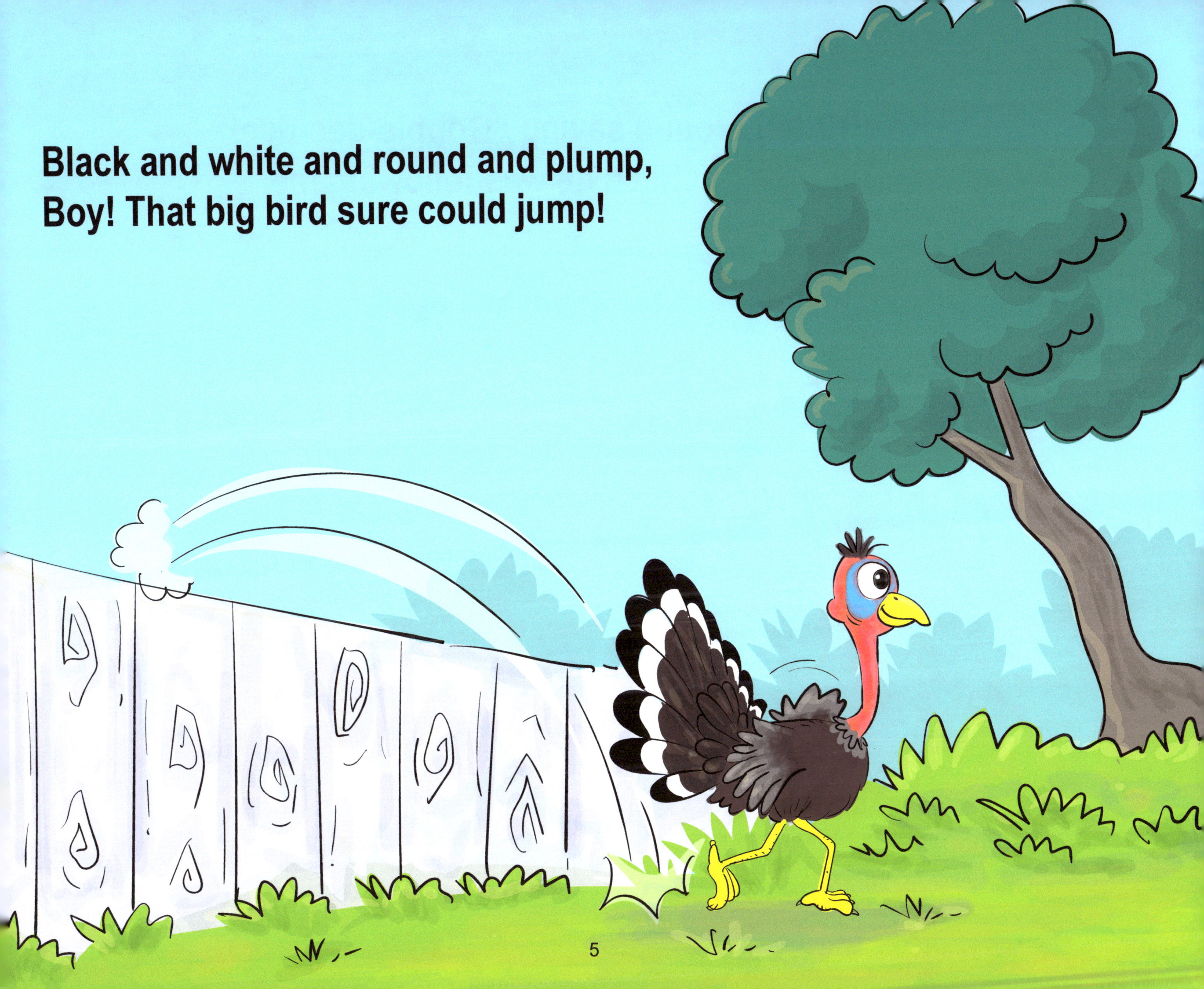

Black and white and round and plump,
Boy! That big bird sure could jump!

He strutted around saying "Gobble-dee-dee!"
But then I noticed he was following me.

Parkway Garden was a mini zoo,
With trails and rabbits and chickens, too.

The front looked like a country store,
And once inside – there was so much more!
Parkway Garden
WELCOME

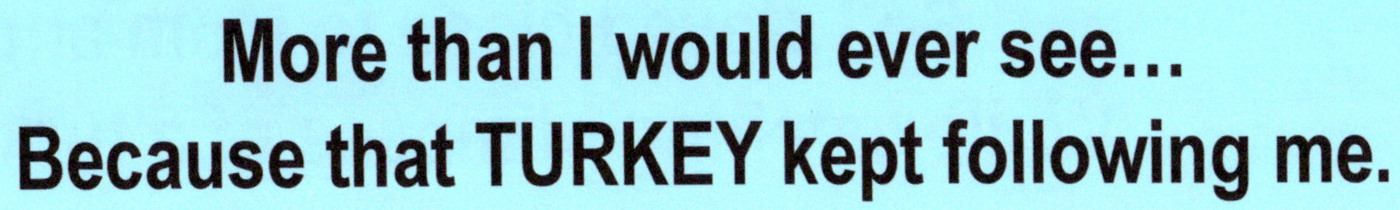

More than I would ever see…
Because that TURKEY kept following me.

So I stayed close to Mom and Gran
While catching glimpses of a turkey tail fan.
Parkway Garden
WELCOME

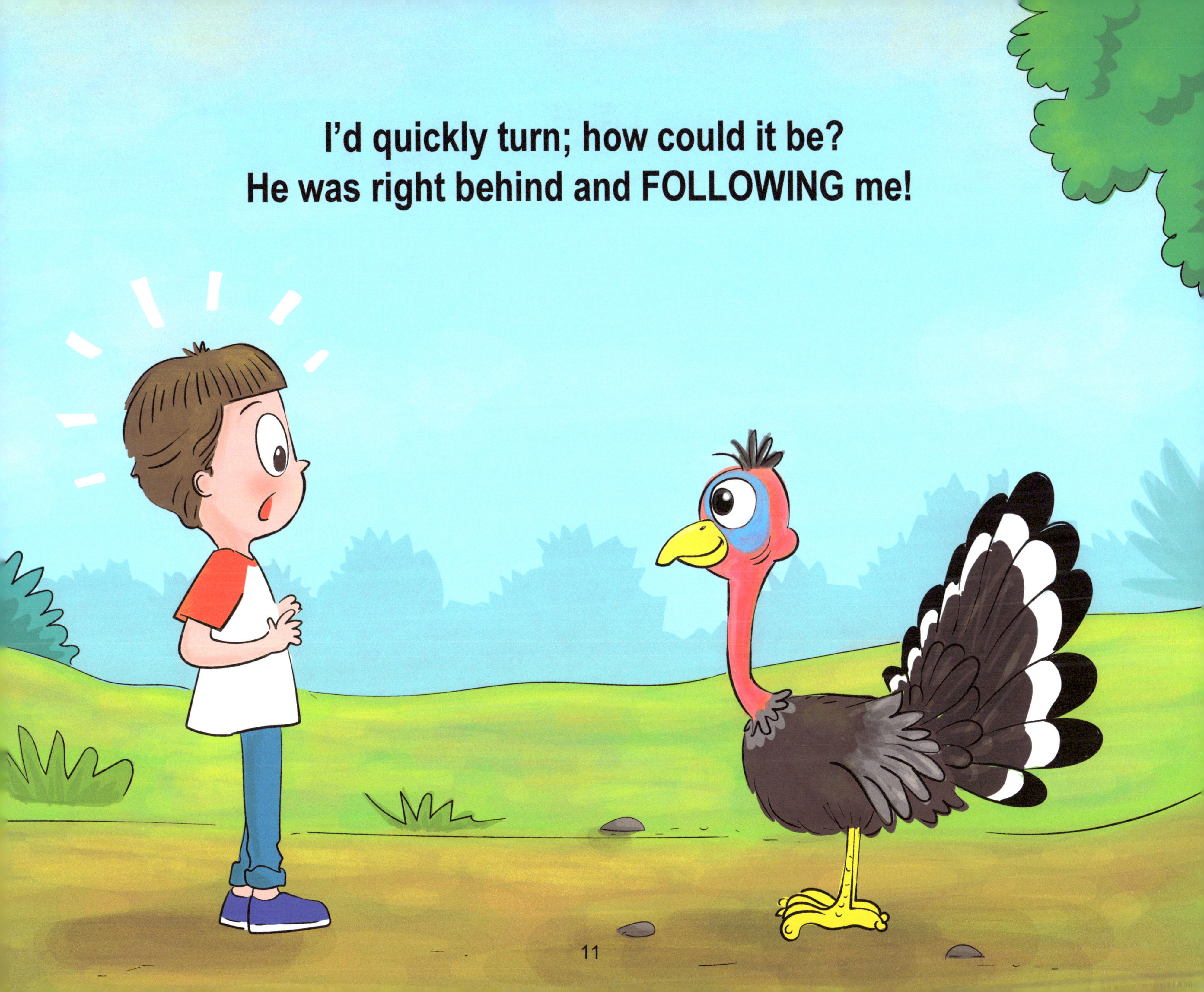

I'd quickly turn; how could it be?
He was right behind and FOLLOWING me!

And he was LAUGHING! Well, how rude!
A turkey with an ATTITUDE.

Everywhere I'd go, every place I'd be
I'd catch that turkey sneaking up on me!

I longed to wander down a trail
But down each trail fanned a turkey's tail!
Right
Left

He put such worry on all my fun
Because I knew that he could run!

And he was FAST! How could it be
That ONE BIG TURKEY was following me!

No place to hide—no space was free…
And why was he only bothering me?

Suddenly, I turned…
… I counted THREE!…

So, the rest of my day
Was FUN INDEED!

An important lesson the Bible teaches is not to become anxious or worried about things.
Worry can waste time, and God doesn't want His children to waste time worrying.
He wants us to talk to Him about everything instead!
These are lessons we learn as we journey through life.
As we grow to understand the importance of reading the Bible,
we discover wonderful truths to help us understand how to live our lives
free from worry while living here on the Earth God created for us.

Philippians 4:6-7 from the New Living Translation (NLT) of the Bible says this:

"Don't worry about anything; instead, pray about everything.
Tell God what you need and thank Him for all He has done.

Then you will experience God's peace, which exceeds anything we can understand.
His peace will guard your hearts and minds as you live in Christ Jesus."

Blessings!
Terry Phillips Griffin

Questions to talk about with your child:

1. Who was the main character in the story?

2. Where was the boy when he first saw the turkey?

3. What did the boy think the turkey was doing?

4. How did the turkey make the boy feel at first?

5. What surprised the boy at the end of the story?

6. How did his feelings change after he saw all three turkeys?

A Prayer When I Feel Worried

Dear God,
Thank You for giving me people I can talk to when I feel worried or confused.
Please help me remember to ask for help when I don't understand what's going on.
And help me to always come to You, because You know everything, and You're always with me!
Thank You for loving me, caring for me, and watching over me every day.
I know I'm never alone because You are always near.

Amen

A Note from Andrew:

Hi, my name is Andrew, and I'm happy to report that I am alive and well after my run-in with the turkeys! This was a true story that happened when I was eight years old. I hope you enjoyed reading it!

Some lessons I've learned since I was young in this story are that no matter how big or intimidating a problem might seem, there's always a way to get through it (just like I did with the turkeys). I've come to realize that our worries are usually nothing to worry about at all. And later, they may even cause us to think back and laugh.

I am now 17 years old, a senior in high school, and I play the drumline at our varsity football games. I hope to attend Texas A&M University soon to pursue a business degree in Finance. I want to spread positivity and the gospel along my journey.

I have a strong relationship with the Lord, and I go to church every Sunday. In my life so far, I believe Christ has shaped me into the man I am today, and I know that His plans for me are wonderful!

Think And Draw

www.ingramcontent.com/pod-product-compliance
Lightning Source LLC
Chambersburg PA
CBHW040108020826

48978CB00019B/144